Thomas

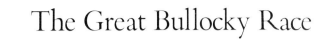

The Great Bullocky Race

First published in the United States in 1988
Published by Dodd, Mead & Company, Inc.
71 Fifth Avenue, New York, N. Y. 10003
Printed by Kyodo, Singapore

1 2 3 4 5 6 7 8 9 10

**Library of Congress Cataloging-in-Publication
Data**

Page, Michael F., date
    The great bullocky race.

    Summary: Two well-known and competitive
Australian bullockies undertake a fierce race, accompanied by their
more peaceable children, to prove their superiority in
driving their teams of cattle.
    [1. Australia — Fiction] I. Ingpen, Robert R., ill.
II. Title.
PZ7.P143Gr   1988   [Fic]   87-15439
ISBN 0-396-09200-4

Originally published in Australia by
Hill of Content Publishing Company Pty Ltd, 1984

The
Great Bullocky
Race

Michael Page and Robert Ingpen

DODD, MEAD & COMPANY · New York

DONALD MACDONALD was the best-known bullocky of the Western District of Victoria and Foxy Murphy was the best-known bullocky of the South-East of South Australia.

Both of them boasted they would take their bullocks anywhere they could find a foothold. Donald said 'My bullocks would climb the Grampians to take fodder to the wallabies. If anyone would pay me for it.'

Foxy said 'If need be my bullocks would swim the Sugarbag Swamp to carry Sunday clothes to the squatters. If anyone would pay me for it.'

Each bullocky had ten bullocks in his team.

Donald's were called Whisky, Heather, Flora, Lomond, Bluebell, Dundee, Kiltie, Roderick, Piper, and Sporran.

Foxy's were called Strawberry, Guinness, Colleen, Shamus, Shawn, Barney, Shamrock, Snowball, Fairy, and Cornie (which was short for Leprechaun).

Both men had very loud voices and whips which cracked like rifleshots.

When people heard a voice in the distance roaring 'Geee-ah, Whisky! Heave away, Kiltie! Put your back into it, Roderick!' they'd tell one another 'Put the kettle on for a cup of tea. Donald Macdonald and his daughter Alice will be here in an hour or so.'

And when people heard a voice yelling 'Pick yer feet up, Shamrock! Heeeeave away, Snowball! Come on, Cornie!' they'd say 'There's Foxy Murphy and his young son Wally coming down the track. They'll be here in an hour or so.'

Donald's daughter Alice had red hair and freckles, and she reckoned she was the only Girl Bullocky in Australia.

Young Wally had been travelling with his father since he was three years old. He reckoned he could handle a bullock team as well as any man twice his size, and he could make his long bullock whip go *Crack-crack-crack*! like rifleshots.

Young Wally had a voice almost as loud as his father's, but Alice's voice was very soft and sweet.

Foxy told his friends 'When Young Wally's voice breaks you'll be able to hear him from Mount Gambier to Bordertown.'

But Alice reckoned that bullocks didn't really like loud voices. She said that when she spoke sweetly and softly in their ears they pulled much harder than when her father roared at them.

Bullockies always had good dogs to help them, to nip at the bullocks' heels and keep them moving along. Donald's dog was called Nipper, and Foxy called his dog Sharkie because of its long teeth.

Donald and Foxy had never met each other, but each of them had heard about the other man.

Donald said 'If ever I meet that Irishman I'll show him how much a real team of bullocks can carry.'

And Foxy said 'If ever I meet that Scotsman I'll show him how fast a real team of bullocks can travel.'

One day more than a hundred years ago, before the railways reached into inland Australia and long before there was any such thing as a motor truck, both Foxy and Donald arrived in the town of Swan Hill on the River Murray.

Swan Hill was a long way out of their usual tracks, but both men had taken on jobs which took them all the way up to the river.

The winter rains and snows had not fallen in the mountains that year, and so the River Murray had almost dried up. The riverboats couldn't run up and down the river, to carry stores to the sheep stations and carry the wool down to the coast for shipment overseas.

So Foxy and Donald had both carried great loads of stores up to the stations along the river.

Their bullock wagons had carried kegs of nails and cases of currants, bags of flour and sacks of sugar, axe handles and hammer heads, boxes of nails and rolls of fencing wire, chests of tea and bales of blankets, stovepipes and tobacco pipes, boots and shoes, bootlaces and necklaces, top hats and felt hats, fishing lines and fish hooks, paint and paintbrushes, ink and writing paper, and a hundred other things needed by people living in the stations along the river.

The station people paid them in golden sovereigns, which they hid away in secret hiding places on their bullock wagons. Then they went to Swan Hill, to load their wagons with bales of wool and carry them down to the seaports.

The stations had all been shearing their sheep, but they couldn't send the wool down the river because it was too dry for the river-boats. The wool bales were stacked up like great square hills and mountains along the riverbank, and a lot of bullock wagons had arrived in Swan Hill to carry them down to the coast.

When Donald and Foxy arrived in Swan Hill, they camped outside the township and went into the pub for a quiet drink of beer. They still hadn't met each other and so Donald didn't know he was drinking in the same pub as the famous Foxy Murphy and Foxy didn't know he was drinking in the same pub as the famous Donald Macdonald.

Just as they sipped at their glasses of beer, a man came into the pub and called out 'I'm told that Australia's two finest bullockies are drinking in this pub and I need to talk to them.'

Donald Macdonald called out 'I'm your man! My bullocks will travel twenty miles a day in any kind of weather!'

And Foxy called out 'I'm your man! *My* bullocks will travel twenty-*two* miles a day with never a pause for breath!'

Donald roared 'Impossible!'

Foxy bellowed ''tis not so! And furthermore I've a wagon eighteen feet long with wheels as high as your head!'

Donald shouted 'My wagon is eighteen feet *six inches* long and my bullocks are all prime four-year-olds!'

Foxy yelled 'They're fit for nothing but fishbait!'

Donald screeched 'Put up your fists! There's no one alive will insult my beautiful bullocks!'

Nipper and Sharkie were waiting outside the pub and as soon as they heard their masters quarrelling they began to fight. They made such a noise that everyone rushed out to see what was happening, and left Donald and Foxy alone with the man who wanted Australia's finest bullockies.

He said 'My name is William McCulloch, and I'm an agent for the woolgrowers. It so happens that Wanganella Station and Clare Station both have urgent loads for London. Each of the stations has grown a fine new breed of wool, and there's a firm in London which wants to buy fifty bales of wool as a sample.'

William McCulloch looked at Donald and Foxy, and said 'But it will only buy fifty bales of wool from *one* of the stations. And it will take the wool that gets there first. There's a clipper ship loading wool at Robe, in South Australia, and it will sail in twenty-one days time. So there's only just time for a bullock wagon to carry the wool down to Robe.'

Donald said 'It's a race — and you can be sure I'll win!'

Foxy shouted 'Nonsense! I'll be there first with the wool!'

Donald took hold of William McCulloch's left arm and Foxy took hold of his right arm and they ran him out of the pub. They both shouted 'Show us where the wool is so I can load it on my wagon, and I'll win the race from Swan Hill to Robe!'

As they hurried Mr McCulloch along the street they met Alice and Young Wally, who had come to see why their fathers were so long at the pub. Donald roared out the story to Alice and Foxy roared it out to Young Wally, so that everyone in town heard about it and called out 'It's a race! It's a race!'

The banker left his bank, the storekeeper left his store, the policeman left his police station, the stableboy left the stables, the grain merchant left his grain, the publican left his pub, the housewives left their houses, and everyone else in town left whatever he or she was doing and followed Donald and Foxy along the street.

When they passed the schoolhouse they made such a noise that Mr Quill the schoolmaster let all the boys and girls out to follow them, and he was just starting to follow the crowd when he thought 'If it's a race they'll need to know where they're going.'

He hurried back into the schoolhouse, took a big map of Australia out of his desk, and ran after the crowd.

Mr McCulloch led the way to the great hills and mountains of wool bales and pointed out two smaller stacks. 'There you are,' he said. 'Wanganella Station and Clare Station hoped to send the wool down the river from Swan Hill, but they didn't know the river had almost dried up.'

Foxy shouted 'I'll take the Wanganella wool and you can be sure Wanganella Station will get the order!'

Donald roared 'Load the Clare wool onto my wagon and you can be certain that Clare Station will get the order!'

The whole crowd cheered them both, and then Mr Quill spoke up. He asked very politely 'Excuse me, gentlemen, but which way will you be going from Swan Hill all the way to Robe?'

Foxy said 'Straight across country as straight as a crow flying home for its dinner!'

Donald said 'Uphill, downhill, across the sand and through the marshes, over the creeks and through the rivers, around the billabongs and the kurrajongs, through the bush and down the gullies, I'll go straight as an arrow all the way to Robe!'

But Mr Quill said 'Excuse me, gentlemen, but it's dry weather and the height of summer, and you'll do better to go a roundabout way to be sure of water for your bullocks.'

He spread out the map and ran his finger across it. He said 'There's your best way. From Swan Hill to Tyntyndyer Station, and across

the creeks to Lake Hindmarsh. Then down south along the Wimmera River until you reach the Glenelg River. Turn west there along the Glenelg River, and then across to Robe through Kadnook, Langkoop, Bool Lagoon, Conmurra and Compurra.'

Mr McCulloch asked 'How do you know so much, Mr Quill?' and he answered modestly 'I'm a schoolmaster and I'm paid for knowing everything.'

Alice looked closely at the map and all the beautiful Aboriginal names on it seemed to make themselves into a kind of poem or song. They made her start singing, and she sang:

> We're off to Robe through Berriwillock
> Goyura and Woomelang.
> We'll be passing by Watchupga
> Tarranyurk and Jeparit.
> One day we'll see Noradjuha
> Toolondo and Kanangulk.
> We'll have dinner at Gringelgalgona
> And afternoon tea at Talangatuck.
> After that it's Natimuk
> Kadnook, Langkoop
> Conmurra, Compurra,
> And then we get to Robe!

Everybody clapped and cheered her, and she said 'Thank you very much, but I'm afraid it doesn't rhyme very well.'

Mr McCulloch said 'H'm, very pretty. But how far is it?'

Mr Quill measured it on his map and said 'I calculate it's near enough four hundred miles. Or if you wanted to make it sound even further than that, you could say six hundred and forty-four kilo-metres.'

Donald said 'My bullocks can travel twenty miles a day and so we shall be there in twenty days.'

Foxy said '*My* bullocks can travel twenty-two miles a day and so we shall be there in eighteen days and a bit.'

Donald roared 'We'll get up earlier every morning and travel further each day!'

Foxy shouted 'We shall travel by the light of the stars!'

Donald bellowed 'We shall never stop to eat!'

Nipper and Sharkie thought there was going to be another fight and they started to growl at each other, but Mr McCulloch said 'You're wasting time with your arguing and there's not a moment to spare.'

Donald and Alice hurried off to their camp to hitch their bullocks to their wagon, and Foxy and Young Wally hurried off to their camp to hitch their bullocks to their wagon. Donald took two golden sovereigns from his secret hiding place in the wagon and told Alice 'You go and buy stores for the trip while I go and load up the wool.'

And Foxy took two golden sovereigns from the secret hiding place in his wagon and said exactly the same thing to Young Wally.

Alice and Young Wally met each other at the store, and found the storekeeper had hurried back there to make sure of their business.

Alice told him 'I want a sack of flour to make damper, and salt and baking powder for the damper, and jam to spread on it, and tea to make billy tea, and potatoes and onions to boil with our salt beef, and pepper and mustard to go with it, and sugar to put in the billy tea, and a new flannel shirt for my father and a new blue ribbon for my hat in case we stop anywhere to go to church on Sundays, and here's two golden sovereigns to pay for everything.'

19

When Young Wally heard her ask for flour for making damper he wished he could ask her how to make it. He and Foxy made the worst damper in Australia. They never managed to make it crisp and brown outside and light and fluffy inside. It was always black and burnt outside and it tasted like rubber inside.

But he was too shy to ask her, and when his turn came he bought the same things as she did except that he bought a new pair of moleskin trousers for his father and a new pair of bootlaces for himself.

The storekeeper gave Alice four pennies, one halfpenny, and one farthing in change from her two golden sovereigns, but he told Young Wally 'There's no change for you because a pair of moleskin trousers costs more than a flannel shirt.'

Then he gave them and their stores a lift in his buggy, because he wanted to see the start of the race. They found that Foxy had loaded his wagon with the Wanganella wool and Donald had loaded his wagon with the Clare Station wool. When they had loaded the stores onto their wagons they were all ready to go.

But Mr McCulloch said 'Just a minute. You can't have a race without proper rules, and I've asked Mr Quill to write out some rules for this race. Read them out, Mr Quill.'

Mr Quill put on his spectacles and read out 'Rule Number One. No dirty tricks, such as one bullocky stealing the wheels off the other bullocky's wagon during the night.'

Donald looked ashamed of himself, as though he'd been thinking of doing just that.

Mr Quill read out 'Rule Number Two. If one bullocky needs help then the other must help him, because you mustn't leave a man in trouble in the bush. But when they're ready to go again, the man who does the helping shall have an hour's start.'

Donald and Foxy nodded agreement, and Mr Quill read out 'Rule Number Three. If one of the bullockies gets drunk on the way, the other bullocky must wait until he gets over it.'

Alice said 'Well I never! I'm sure *I* shan't get drunk.'

Young Wally said 'Nor me neither.'

Donald and Foxy said nothing. They just looked up at the sky.

Mr McCulloch said 'Right, those are the rules. Get ready to go.'

Donald and Alice led their bullocks round so that Whisky and Heather, who led the team, were facing along the road out of town. Foxy and Young Wally led their bullocks round so that Strawberry and Guinness, were level with Whisky and Heather.

For a few minutes all four bullockies bustled around the bullocks and the wagons to make sure that the bullocks' collars were comfortable, and that the chains leading from the collars to the wagon poles weren't too tight, and that the ropes holding the huge towering stacks of wool onto the wagons were tied firmly.

Then Mr McCulloch held up his hand and shouted 'One to get ready . . . two to make steady . . . and three for the OFF!'

Nipper and Sharkie barked and nipped at the bullocks' heels. Donald and Foxy and Young Wally cracked their whips like rifleshots. Donald roared out in a huge voice that frightened the chickens all over town. 'Geeee-ahhh, Whisky! Heave away, Heather!'

And Foxy roared out in a voice that frightened the pelicans off the river and made them all fly into the air. 'Giddap, Strawberry and Guinness! Giddalong, Colleen and Shamus!'

Young Wally made his whip go *Crack-crack-crack*! as the bullocks began to move, very slowly at first as they heaved at the big wagons with their loads of wool, and then moving a little faster and a little faster. The big wagon wheels creaked and groaned along the dusty street, the bullock chains clinked, and the woodwork of the wagons squeaked and squealed under the weight.

On the main street of Swan Hill the two wagons could go side by side, with the townspeople running and cheering around them. But when they left the town, Donald and Foxy could see that the track to Tyntyndyer Station was only wide enough for one bullock wagon at a time.

They both wanted to be first on the track and they cracked their whips and shouted louder than ever. Alice walked alongside Donald's team and spoke softly and sweetly into their ears, saying 'Try hard, Bluebell. Pull harder, Dundee. Heave away, Piper and Sporran.'

But there was a man in the crowd who had a new penny-farthing bicycle. He couldn't ride it very well but he was very proud of it. He rode in front of Foxy's team with his legs going round like a windmill, and then his big front wheel hit a stone and he went *wallop* in the dust in front of Strawberry and Guinness. The two bullocks stopped walking in case they trod on him, and this gave Donald just enough time to get ahead and be the first on the track.

The day was hot and the townsfolk soon went home, but the two bullock wagons creaked on and on with their big wheels rumbling and grumbling in the dust. When the sun started to go down, Alice asked Donald 'Aren't we going to stop and camp for the night?'

He said 'If we stop, Foxy will get ahead of us.'

And Foxy told Young Wally 'We can't stop until Donald stops, or he'll get too far ahead of us.'

Probably they would both have carried on all through the night, each of them waiting for the other to be first to stop. But when the sun went down, the bullocks simply stopped walking because they couldn't see the way ahead. Donald and Foxy had to turn them loose for the night, and tie bullock bells around their necks so that they could find them in the morning, while Alice and Young Wally made camp and built fires and cooked dinner for their fathers.

They all ate their dinners and went to sleep, while Nipper and Sharkie kept watch by their masters' fires. Soon, the two dogs heard a strange sound from the bush.

From one part of the bush came a howling noise that sounded like *Dingohhhhhhh . . . dingowwwwwwww . . . dingoooooohhhhhhhh . . .*

And another part of the bush answered *Dingowwwwwwww . . .*

And another part howled *Dingooooooooohhhhhhhh . . .*'

Nipper jumped up from the fire and trotted across to Sharkie, and said to him in dog talk *Those are dingoes.*

Sharkie said *I know. They'll try to catch one of the bullocks.*

Nipper said *If I go after them by myself, they'll all jump on me and eat me.*

Sharkie said *Then you go one way and I'll go another. If we both make a lot of noise they'll think we're a whole pack of dogs.*

So the two dogs ran into the bush, barking and snarling and making so much noise that the dingoes thought they were a whole pack of fierce bullock dogs and ran away. Donald and Alice and Foxy and Young Wally were all sound asleep and didn't hear any of this, but in the morning they noticed that the two dogs had made friends. Sometimes they walked together under Donald's wagon and sometimes under Foxy's wagon, to keep out of the sun.

The bullocks pulled the wagons along very slowly, less than four kilometres an hour, with the steel tyres on the great wooden wheels grinding through the dust. Donald and Foxy and Young Wally walked by the wagons, with their long whips trailing in the dust. Alice walked by herself, singing softly as she looked at the beautiful bush and listened to the songs of the magpies.

The day went slowly by, the sun rose higher and higher and then started to slide down the sky, the wagons squeaked and groaned along, and Donald was beginning to think about his dinner when a boy rode suddenly out of the bush ahead of them. He was riding a black donkey, and he pointed a pistol at them and shouted 'Bail up! Bail up! I'm Beezelbub the Boy Bushranger and this is my gallant steed Midnight! Bail up!'

Alice said 'You mean Beelzebub, don't you? Not Beezelbub.'

'It doesn't make any difference how you say it. I'm Beezelbub the Boy Bushranger, the Terror of the Riverlands — or at least I will be when I grow up. Bail up!'

Donald thought of his secret store of gold sovereigns hidden in his wagon, and said 'But bushrangers aren't supposed to hold up bull-

ock wagons. You ought to hold up stagecoaches.'

Beezelbub the Boy Bushranger said 'I've got to practise some-where. Bail up!'

Alice took out the money that the storekeeper gave her in change for two golden sovereigns, and said 'We've only got fourpence three-farthings.'

'That'll do to begin with. Bring it over here.'

She walked over to him, but as she went closer she said 'Why, your pistol is only a wooden one, painted black.'

Beezelbub said 'Oh rats! Just like a girl to spoil everything!'

Foxy, like Donald, was thinking of his dinner, and he called out 'Get off your gallant steed and have a bite to eat with us.'

Beezelbub said 'Thank you kindly, and you can call me Bub for short.' He stepped off Midnight and let go the reins (which were only made of string) and Midnight quickly bolted off into the bush. Beezelbub said 'Oh rats! Now I'll have to walk home and I'll be late for the milking.'

He went over to have dinner with Foxy and Young Wally, and Young Wally gave him a piece of damper spread with melon and lemon jam. Bub took a bite and said 'Ugh! This is the worst damper I ever tasted!'

Then Young Wally gave him a plate of dinner, but when he

began to eat it he said 'Pheugh! The salt beef is hard, the potatoes are almost raw, and the onions aren't cooked properly. Even your billy tea tastes terrible.'

He jumped up and said 'I've lost my gallant steed, my pistol doesn't fool anyone, I've got to walk all the way home for the milking, and you can't even give me a decent dinner. If I was Ned Kelly I'd — I'd shoot the horns off your lead bullocks!'

He ran down the track and into the bush, but just before they lost sight of him he called out 'Beware Snake Gully!'

They didn't know what he meant, but Foxy said to Young Wally 'He's right, you know. Our grub does taste terrible. I reckon it's time you learned to cook.'

Young Wally said 'Me? But who's going to teach me?'

Foxy thought a bit and then he said 'Why don't you ask Alice? The smell of their dinner always makes my mouth water.'

So Young Wally went over to Alice and asked her how to make damper, and she showed him how but he couldn't get the hang of it. She said 'Come back again tomorrow night.'

When they were ready to start next morning, Donald came over to Foxy and said 'You've got to give us an hour's start this morning, on account of Alice helped you by giving Young Wally a cooking lesson.'

Foxy had to agree, and when the sun went down that night he was almost three kilometres behind Donald. But he still told Young Wally to walk along for his cooking lesson, and next morning he had to give Donald another hour's start. The same thing happened on the next night, and the next night, and the night after that, and by that time Donald Macdonald's wagon was so far ahead that Wally had to walk a long long way to his wagon and back again to have his cooking lesson. But Foxy said 'Never mind. We'll catch up with them. And you're making good damper at last.'

Next morning, Young Wally made the best damper that Foxy had ever tasted. It was brown and crisp on the outside and light and fluffy on the inside, and Foxy ate three-quarters of it all by himself. After that, he went into the bush to round up his bullocks. They'd had a good drink out of a creek, and a good feed of dry grass and tender leaves, and then each of them found a shady tree and stood underneath it. They all wished that Foxy would give them a day off, and stood very still so that he couldn't find them. But now and again they moved a bit and then the bullock bells round their necks went *tonk-tonk-tonk* and Foxy could find them quite easily.

They started off again down the track, and they hadn't gone far when they saw a cloud of dust ahead of them. Foxy said 'That's strange. Donald's had six hours start on us by this time, and you'd

34

think he'd be much further down the track.'

Soon they caught up with Donald's wagon and saw it was moving very slowly. Donald told them 'I reckon we found that Snake Gully that Beezelbub was talking about. We camped in this nice shady gully but then we found it was full of snakes. Black snakes, brown snakes, tiger snakes — every kind of snake you can think of. Alice and I had to sleep on top of the wagon, but seven of my bullocks were bitten during the night.'

Foxy said 'A snake bite will never kill a bullock, though.'

Donald said 'No, but look how they're limping along.'

Foxy said 'I'll soon cure that. I'll give them a dose of Old Wally's Famous Snakebite Cure, that was invented by Young Wally's grandfather. It's made of whisky, turpentine, kerosene, red pepper, linseed oil, eucalyptus oil, and horse liniment, and I've never known it to fail. Not on bullocks, that is. It's not so good for humans.'

He got the bottle from his wagon and gave the first dose to Sporran, who coughed, snorted, kicked up his heels, and tried to pull the wagon all by himself. Then he gave doses to the other bullocks who'd been bitten by snakes. Kiltie licked his lips as though he'd like some more, Piper tried to crack his tail like a bullock whip, Dundee jumped right off the ground, Bluebell and Lomond bellowed *Bawwwwwww*, and Roderick rolled his big brown eyes.

Donald said 'Thank you very kindly, and we'll be on our way.'

Foxy said 'Just a moment, now. You owe me an hour's start. You've had six hours start on me, but now I've helped you seven times. That wipes out the six hours and gives me an hour's start.'

Donald scratched his head but he couldn't argue with that. He had to pull his wagon aside so that Foxy could go by, and then Alice boiled the billy for a cup of tea. Donald said 'We'll never catch up now,' but when the hour had passed he found that Old Wally's Famous Snakebite Cure had made his bullocks so lively that they caught up with Foxy before the end of the day.

The two wagons camped side by side, and after dinner Young Wally went across to see Alice. Foxy called out 'Don't you have no

more cooking lessons, now, or we'll lose another hour's start.'

But Young Wally said 'I'm just going over to talk to her. We both want to have bullock wagons when we grow up, and we've decided we might as well have one wagon and share it between us.'

Foxy snuggled down in his swag and grumbled 'Stone the crows. First my dog makes friends with Donald's dog, then my boy makes friends with Donald's girl. Next thing I know, my bullocks will make friends with Donald's bullocks, and then I suppose I shall have to make friends with Donald.'

Next morning, the bells of twenty bullocks went *tonk-tonk-tonk* in the bush, and they didn't even have to go out to round them up. Nipper and Sharkie raced off into the bush and nipped at the bullocks' heels until they hurried out to be harnessed to the wagons.

The days passed by as the wagons moved slowly along the track, to Lake Hindmarsh and then southwards down the Wimmera River. They followed the tracks made by other bullock wagons whenever they could, winding between the little towns and stations along the way. Often these tracks didn't run directly south, but it was easier to follow them than to make new tracks of their own.

Sometimes the tracks were wide and smooth, sometimes they were very narrow and rough. Sometimes they went down into deep gullies and up the other side. Sometimes the dust was so thick that it sifted like flour over the wagon wheels, and sometimes the track was covered with rocks and stones. And sometimes they couldn't find a track which led the way they wanted to go, and so they had to make a new track of their own.

They would talk about the best way to go, and Alice went ahead to find the best way through. She kept her eye on the sun to make sure she was going in the right direction. Foxy and Donald followed with axes, to cut down small trees that stood in the way. Young Wally took charge of both bullock teams, making his whip go *Crack-crack-crack*! like rifleshots and roaring at the bullocks as loudly as his dad. The huge wheels of the wagons went grinding and crushing through the bush, and made tracks that other people could follow for years to come.

Sometimes the wagons passed through little townships along the track, and people came blinking and yawning out of their houses to watch them creaking and groaning and rumbling and grumbling by, with Nipper and Sharkie barking and Young Wally cracking his whip.

In one township a man asked Foxy where he was going, and Foxy said 'We're running the Great Bullocky Race all the way from Swan Hill on the Murray to Robe in South Australia.'

The man said 'That's the slowest race I've ever seen. A man could

go to sleep watching a race like that,' and he went back into his house and went to sleep again.

The Wimmera River had dried up into pools and waterholes, but there was enough water to keep the bullocks going. The worst problem was finding enough feed. Other bullock teams had eaten most of the feed along the Wimmera, and the bullocks belonging to Foxy and Donald became hungrier and hungrier and walked more and more slowly. They had to go further and further into the bush each evening to find enough to eat, and Nipper and Sharkie had to spend a long time rounding them up each morning.

Donald told Alice 'We've only got half the way to Robe, and our bullocks are only walking fifteen miles a day.'

And Foxy told Young Wally 'If we go on like this, we'll stop.'

But late one day the two wagons passed some big paddocks full of long thick grass. It was as crisp and crunchy as the dampers that Young Wally made after Alice's cooking lessons, but it was all fenced off from the track.

The bullocks' mouths watered when they saw it, and Foxy walked back to Donald and said 'If the bullocks could have a feed of that good grass they'd soon get going again.'

Before Donald could answer him they saw a man riding towards them on a big black horse. He reined up and said 'Now, you bullockies, keep your eyes off of my grass. I'm Ebenezer Handy of Paddywallock Station, and all that grass belongs to me.'

Foxy said 'We'll pay you well for it, boss. Our bullocks are very hungry.'

Ebenezer Handy said 'Even if Queen Victoria came driving a bullock team down this track I wouldn't sell my grass to her. I need it all for my sheep.'

He dug his spurs in his big black horse and galloped away. Foxy looked at Donald and said 'Anyway, he can't stop us camping on the track for the night.'

So they made their camps as the sun went down, and lit their fires and cooked their dinners. When it was dark they could hear all the bullocks moving about, and Foxy told Young Wally 'I reckon Strawberry and Guinness might be strong enough to break down the fences round that grass.'

They went on eating their dinners, and soon they heard a crunching munching sound from the paddocks. Donald told Alice 'Well I never. If Ebenezer Handy hadn't told us that our bullocks mustn't eat his grass, I could swear I can hear them eating it.'

And when Foxy got up in the morning he said 'Well I never. The bullocks must have broken down the fences in the night, and they've all had a good feed of that lovely long dry grass.'

Just then, Mr Ebenezer Handy came galloping down the track on his big black horse. He waved his horsewhip round his head and shouted 'You rascals! You villains! You ruffians! Your bullocks have broken down my fences and gobbled up a whole lot of my grass!'

Donald went to the secret hiding place on his wagon and took out two golden sovereigns, and Foxy took two golden sovereigns from the secret place on his wagon. The sun shone and sparkled on the golden coins when they held them out to Mr Handy, and he said 'Well I never. Those four golden sovereigns will just about pay for all the grass that's been gobbled up out of my paddocks.'

The bullocks had had such a good supper and breakfast that they pulled more strongly than ever, and the bullock wagons rumbled and creaked and groaned south from the Wimmera River until they met the Glenelg River, and then turned west towards Kadnook, Langkoop, Conmurra, Compurra, and Robe.

There had been good winter rains along the Glenelg River and so there was plenty of feed, and the bullocks rolled their big brown eyes with pleasure when they were set free every night.

Foxy told Young Wally 'We'll soon be in our own part of the country, the South-East of South Australia. I'll bet you we can leave Donald and Alice far behind and win the race.'

Donald told Alice 'Foxy is still moving a bit faster than we are but I'll bet you we can catch up with him and win the race.'

After dinner that night, Alice met Young Wally in the bush, under the big shining moon and the thousands of stars that shone like silver lanterns. They met like that on most nights and talked over their plans to have their own bullock wagon when they were grown up. Alice said 'I don't know what dad will do if he loses this race. He'll think it's a terrible disgrace.'

And Young Wally said 'I don't know what *my* dad will do if *he* loses the race. He's set his heart on winning it.'

Alice said 'If dad loses it, I think he'll forbid me to talk to you ever again.'

Young Wally said 'Oh dear.'

Next day they set off on a clear shining morning, but Foxy sniffed the air and said 'I reckon there's rain about somewhere.'

A great storm had gathered far away to the north-west, above the deserts where bullock wagons had never travelled, and soon the great black clouds came rolling down across the sky and covered up the sun. Thunder crashed and roared and the rain poured down so heavily that the bullocks could hardly see.

The track looked more like a creek, with water running fast along it. The bullocks' rough coats were slicked down by the rain, and water poured off the great stacks of wool bales. The huge wheels of the wagons squelched and splashed through the muddy water of the track.

Foxy and Young Wally and Donald and Alice plodded along beside the wagons, wet and miserable. It was so wet that Young Wally couldn't make his whip go *Crack-crack-crack*! like rifleshots.

But the rain stopped and the sun came out again, and they felt more cheerful until they came to a creek running across the track. The rain had been so heavy that the creek was roaring along as brown as billy tea, sweeping along branches and leaves and even a small tree trunk now and again.

Foxy said 'It might take a day or two for this creek to go down, and if we wait here we'll miss the ship.'

They stared at the rushing water and scratched their heads, until Young Wally said 'One team of bullocks wouldn't be strong enough to pull a wagon through. It would just be swept away. But if we hitched both teams of bullocks to one wagon and pulled it across, and then hitched both teams to the other wagon, I think we could make it.'

Donald said 'But then we'd be helping each other, and we'd have to give each other an hour's start.'

Alice said 'Of course we wouldn't. It means that you'd give Foxy an hour's start, and he'd give you an hour's start, and so you'd both

start off at the same time.'

Donald said 'Oh yes. I never thought of that.'

Foxy said 'Come on. We're wasting time.'

He and Young Wally unhitched all his bullocks and led them around to hitch onto Donald's team. The two teams of bullocks were good friends by that time because they'd spent so many nights in the bush together. They stood quietly until they were all hitched up into a twenty-bullock team, and then Young Wally made his whip go *Crack-crack-crack*! while Foxy roared 'Gee-ah, Strawberry and Guinness!' and Donald roared 'Heave away, Whisky! Giddap, Heather and Roderick!'

Alice walked beside the long team, talking softly into the ears of Foxy's bullocks as well as those of Donald's bullocks. She told them to do their best and not to be afraid of the rushing water.

Slipping and sliding, the bullocks went down the bank into the roaring creek. It almost swept Strawberry and Guinness off their feet, but they kept bravely on and then Colleen and Shamus, Shawn and Barney, and all the other bullocks followed after them.

The wagon splashed into the creek and the water foamed up around it but didn't reach the wool. Young Wally plunged into the creek and pulled himself across by the side of the wagon and the bodies of the bullocks, and led them up the steep bank on the other side. All twenty of them heaved as hard as they could and pulled the wagon clear, sploshing and squelching with water pouring off its huge wheels.

Then he led the bullocks back to pull the other wagon across, with Alice sitting on top of the wool so that she wouldn't get wet. Donald and Foxy had to hang on behind and when they got across the creek the water poured out of their clothes and boots.

After that they followed the track with their clothes steaming dry in the sun. The days went by as the bullocks walked along the track across the plains and around the hills and along the limestone ridges which cross the swamps of the South-East. One morning, Foxy said 'I reckon I can smell the sea! We'll be in Robe tomorrow!'

The bullocks plodded on and the huge wheels squeaked and groaned. The sun began to go down, and they saw the light of camp-fires a little way ahead of them. When they reached the fires they saw a lot of bullock wagons standing in a gully, with bullocks feeding on the slopes around them.

Foxy said 'We've come to Drunkards Gully, where all the bullockies stop for a drink on their way back home from Robe. We'd better make camp here for the night.'

When they made camp, the other bullockies came up and talked to them. Donald and Foxy met a lot of old friends, such as Four-

Finger Nick from Geelong and Terrible Ted from Tantanoola and Dismal Dick from Dinglebledinga. They all said to Foxy and Donald 'You'd better have a drink, mates. You look as though you've travelled a long way.'

Foxy and Donald had so many drinks with their old mates that they couldn't get up in the morning. Foxy told Young Wally 'Let me sleep it off for a bit' and Donald told Alice 'I'll be all right in a few hours time.'

Alice said to Young Wally 'What are we going to do? It's the twenty-first day, and the ship will sail without any of the wool. And Rule Number Three said that if one bullocky gets drunk, the other must give him time to get better.'

Young Wally thought a minute, and said 'The rule doesn't say that you and I can't carry on with the race. I'll help you hitch up your bullocks and we'll carry on.'

So they started again, and went down the long winding road into Robe. They could see the sailing ships at anchor, and young Wally made his whip go *Crack-crack-crack*! while Alice spoke softly into the ears of the bullocks and said 'Hurry up, Lomond. Pull hard, Bluebell. We'll miss the ship if you don't hurry up.'

But the two teams of bullocks had become so friendly that none of them wanted to go faster than the others. They walked side by side down the main street of Robe, with all the people running out to cheer them on, and then up to the roundabout called Royal Circus. And there they stopped, with Whisky and Heather exactly level with Strawberry and Guinness.

The captain of the ship was waiting for them there and he waved his cap as the two wagons stopped side by side. 'You're just in time,' he said. 'My boats are waiting to carry the wool out to the ship and then I'm sailing for London.'

Alice asked him 'But how will you know which load of wool to carry to London? We both got here at the same time.'

The captain said 'It doesn't matter. A ship came in yesterday with a letter from London, telling me to carry all the wool from both stations in my ship. So it's lucky you both got here together.'

Just then, Foxy and Donald came down the street and up to Royal Circus. They looked at the wagons standing side by side, and they both asked together 'But who won the Great Bullocky Race?'

And Alice and Young Wally said together 'We both did!'